# Scientist, Scientist,
## Who Do You See?

A Scientific Parody
by Chris Ferrie

sourcebooks
jabberwocky

Copyright © 2018 by Chris Ferrie
Cover and internal design © 2018 by Allison Sundstrom/Sourcebooks, Inc.
Cover and internal illustrations by Chris Ferrie

Sourcebooks and the colophon are registered trademarks of Sourcebooks, Inc.

This book is a parody and has not been prepared, approved, or authorized by the creators of
*Brown Bear, Brown Bear, What Do You See?* or their heirs or representatives.

Published by Sourcebooks Jabberwocky, an imprint of Sourcebooks, Inc.
P.O. Box 4410, Naperville, Illinois 60567-4410
(630) 961-3900
Fax: (630) 961-2168
sourcebooks.com

Library of Congress Cataloging-in-Publication Data is on file with the publisher.

Source of Production: RR Donnelley, Shenzhen, Guangdong Province, China
Date of Production: January 2018
Run Number: 5011067

Printed and bound in China.
RRD 10 9 8 7 6 5 4 3 2 1

Einstein,
Einstein,
Who do you see?

I see Marie Curie
in her laboratory.

Curie,
Curie,
Who do you see?

I see Ahmed Zewail pioneering laser chemistry.

Zewail,
Zewail,
Who do you see?

I see Grace Hopper
making a computer enquiry.

Hopper,
Hopper,
Who do you see?

I see James Maxwell
with magnets and electricity.

Maxwell,
Maxwell,
Who do you see?

I see Ada Lovelace
writing computer code for thee.

Lovelace,
Lovelace,
Who do you see?

I see George Carver studying botany.

Carver,
Carver,
Who do you see?

I see Chien-Shiung Wu experimenting carefully.

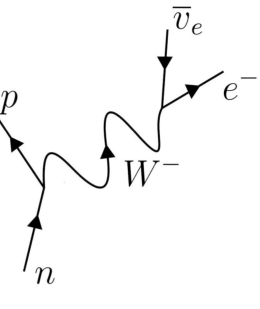

**Wu,
Wu,
Who do you see?**

I see Alan Turing
inventing computer theory.

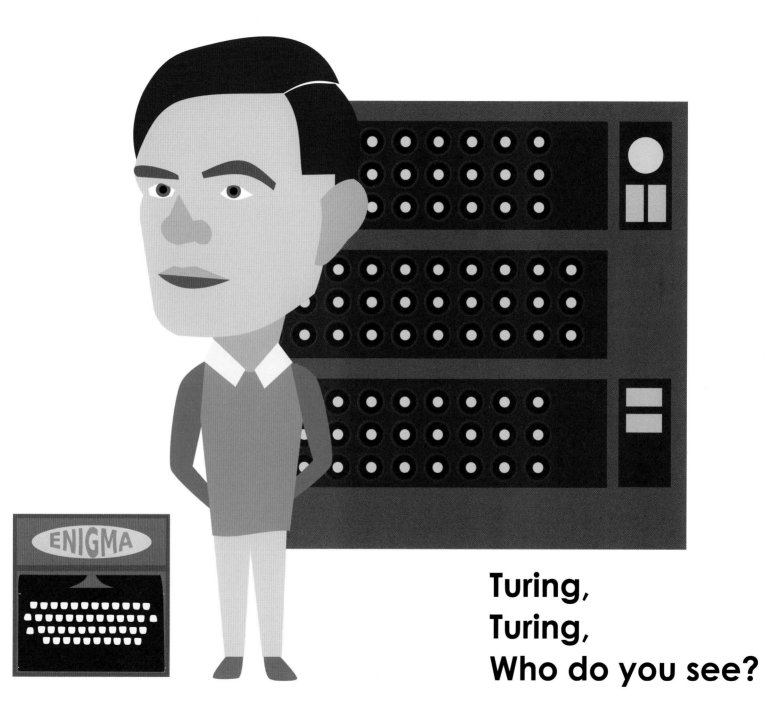

Turing,
Turing,
Who do you see?

I see Anna Mani
studying meteorology.

Mani,
Mani,
Who do you see?

I see Charles Darwin
and the diversity of species.

Darwin,
Darwin,
Who do you see?

I see Katherine Johnson solving analytic geometry.

Johnson,
Johnson,
Who do you see?

I see little scientists looking at me.

**Scientists,
Scientists,
Who do you see?**

Albert Einstein,     Marie Curie,     Ahmed Zewail,

Grace Hopper,     James Maxwell,     Ada Lovelace,

**George Washington Carver,**

**Chien-Shiung Wu,**

**Alan Turing,**

**Anna Mani,**

**Charles Darwin,**

**and Katherine Johnson
looking at us. That's what we see!**

# About the Scientists

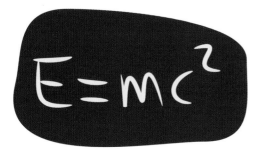

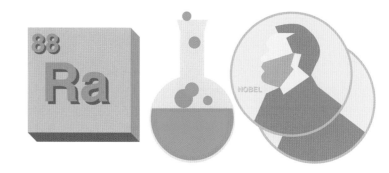

**Albert Einstein** is one of history's most famous scientists. He worked on many areas of physics, but is most known for his theory of relativity.

**Marie Curie** is the only person to have won two different Nobel prizes in science. She did so for her work in Physics and Chemistry.

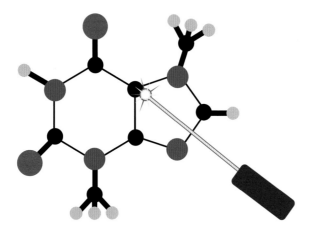

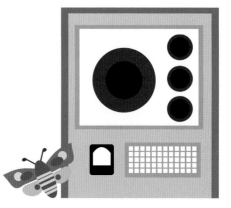

**Ahmed Zewail** was an award-winning chemist. He used very very very short laser pulses to watch chemical reactions happening.

**Grace Hopper** invented the first computer compiler. She was a U.S. Rear Admiral, and was one of the first programmers on early supercomputers.

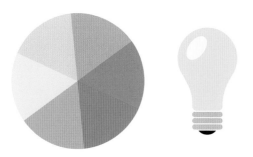

**James Maxwell** was a physicist known for his work on electromagnetism and thermodynamics. He also created the first color photograph.

**Ada Lovelace** was a mathematician who published the first algorithm for a real computer in 1843. She is considered the first computer programmer.

**George Washington Carver** was a botanist born into slavery. His research on crops and soil led to larger yields of peanuts and other foods.

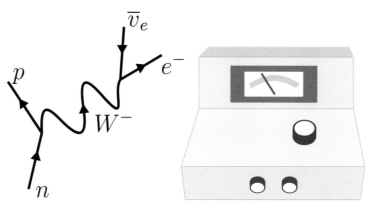

**Chien-Shiung Wu** was an experimental scientist whose work in nuclear physics resolved many questions in quantum physics. She was the first ever female instructor hired at Princeton University.

**Alan Turing** founded the field of computer science and artificial intelligence. He also helped end WWII by breaking enemy codes.

**Anna Mani** was both a physicist and a meteorologist. She developed and studied new tools of measuring solar and wind energy.

**Charles Darwin** was a naturalist famous for his theory of evolution, which explains the diversity of life by natural selection.

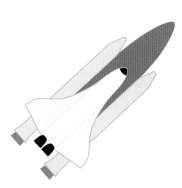

**Katherine Johnson** is known for groundbreaking work in mathematics and physics that enabled NASA to use computers to calculate flight paths in space.

**Chris Ferrie** is a physicist and mathematician. He is the author of this book as well as *Goodnight Lab* and *Quantum Physics for Babies*.

**And finally, YOU!** You can be the next person to change the world. There are so many questions left. What will your answer be?